The *South* Pole Reindeer Revolt

By

Rodney Norman

DEDICATION

For my wonderful family who always believed.

ACKNOWLEDGMENTS

This story was written at the request of my children. Thank you Candace, Alyssa and Blair. I love you with all my heart.   Thank you Lisa for your artwork, your unwavering support of me in whatever I do and being the best wife a man could ask for in this world. I could not have done this without you. I would like to thank my mother who always wanted me to follow my dreams and my father who taught me the value of integrity and hard work. I would also like to thank Ms Linda Roseberry for her guidance.

    The wind was blowing and snow was flying all around. Rocky squinted at the tiny light visible from the distant tent. Rocky bore his hooves against the snowy ice and trudged ahead to investigate. He lowered his antlers and got his body as close to the ice as he could.

    "Can't let um see me," he thought. He moved slowly to what appeared to be some sort of igloo made from cloth. It was red and black, and in front of the igloo was a pole with another piece of cloth tied to it with a string. He put his ear up to the igloo and listened.

    "I am sure glad we got this new tent. The last one didn't keep the cold out like this one does." a voice said.

"Yeah Marv, it does, but this is not what I imagined my Christmas would be like. I mean, how lucky are we to have to spend Christmas in the *South* Pole. When Charles told us we had outpost duty, I almost threw up. I mean, we are on the complete opposite side of where Santa is." the other voice said.

"Well Henry, it could be worse. No! What am I saying? It couldn't be. My kids are probably putting out the cookies and candy for Santa and the reindeer right now." Marv said with a sigh.

"Hey, I know what we should do!" exclaimed Marv. "Let's open the cards our kids gave us before we left."

"Yeah! That is a great idea!" Henry shot back with excitement. "Then we will go to sleep, and get up in the morning and open presents."

Marv reached into his faded green bag and pulled out several envelopes. He handed two to Henry and kept the three from his children. Rocky became even more curious as to what the two men were doing. He leaned forward even more to get a peek inside. Unfortunately, his antlers snagged on one of the strings on the tent, and when he moved, it opened the window to the tent, letting the harsh wind in. Everything inside the tent blew around and Marv and Henry bumbled to get their coats. They went outside to see what was going on. All they found was a broken string and some fur. They quickly tied the tent back down and went back inside puzzled at what could have broken the string.

Rocky was off like a flash, running as fast as his hooves would take him. He had to get back. He had to show his friends what he discovered. He held on to the envelopes in his mouth as tight as he could, knowing his friends would find them as interesting as he did.

When he arrived back home, his friends were doing their usual activities, which in his mind were all unimportant, but extremely predictable. Tut-tut was looking at a tuft of grass poking out of the snow, and trying to say, "Tuft" without stuttering at it. Candy was using the snow and ice to make sure not a speck of dirt was found in her perfect fur. Eugene was puzzling over the reason the glacier was getting smaller, and trying to put together a theory he called "Glacier Warming." Borris was trying, without much success, to ignore them all. Meteor and Laggy were playing chase and Laggy was ALWAYS "it". Servile was going around to each of them, trying to remember whom it was that wanted to play hide and go seek. Solo was the one that wanted to play, because no one could ever find him, but Servile had forgotten that. Solo was nowhere to be found, but that did not surprise Rocky at all. Rocky took in a deep breath.

"LISTEN UP, LADIES!" He shouted in a very loud voice. "We have a problem. Something has come to my attention that you should all know about."

"What!? That you are moving, and will never be around to give us another boring speech?" Borris said with a snicker.

"W-w-w-w-hat is it-t-t-t?" asked Tut-tut.

Meteor ran up to Rocky before Tut-tut had even finished his first word. He looked at what Rocky had laid on the ground and started jumping and running around the whole place.

"I have come to find out that we are not getting what we deserve. Have a look at these," reported Rocky.

Rocky pulled out the colorful envelopes and took the cards from inside them. Each card had Santa Claus pulling his sleigh, and on one, it even had a picture of reindeer getting candy canes. The title of the card with the reindeer getting candy was "Merry Christmas from the North Pole".

"Ss-s-o w-w-w-Whut-tt-t g-g-g-gives?" Tut-tut asked.

"I think these reindeer of the north have lived the good life long enough. They aren't any better than we are. We need to go up there and show these high and mighty reindeer that we can pull Santa's sled just as good as they can. NOW, WHO'S WITH ME?" Rocky exclaimed.

"Well, count me out." Borris stated without much thought.

"I w-w-w-ill g-g-g-go." muttered Tut-tut.

"WOW! Like, oh my gosh! Will you look at those cute gold bells and matching sleigh! I am like, so totally in! Those reindeer must get brushed and bathed every day to look like that!" giggled Candy with delight.

"I would love to go. This way I can see just how far the problem of "Glacier Warming" has spread." Eugene said.

"I............will................go." Laggy said, while everyone stared at how extremely long it took him to finish his statement.

"What are we talking about again?" asked Servile, who had obviously forgotten.

"Going up to the North Pole and showing those spoiled reindeer that they don't have anything on us South Pole reindeer." reminded Rocky with a loud exhale.

"Oh! Ok, well I will go. Where is it exactly that we are going?" asked Servile in a low voice.

"TO THE NORTH POLE!" yelled Rocky making Servile back up into Borris.

"I am so going now. I have completely changed my mind." said Borris in a very determined tone.

"Great, Borris, what made you change your mind? The fact that it is a worthy cause and a chance for us South Pole reindeer to finally get some well deserved credit?" Rocky swelled as he asked.

"No, I just like the opportunity to see you guys yell, get upset, and eventually fail and come home. I can't miss that for anything!" Borris laughed.

"I wanna go! I wanna go! I wanna go! I want to be in front!" Meteor kept saying so fast that he was barely understandable.

"You m-m-m-must b-b-b-be kk-k-idding? YYYou w-w-wwould p-pull too f-f-fast" Tut-tut interjected.

"Where is Solo? I am sure he will stay here." Rocky said looking around.

"Actually," Solo said as he walked from behind Rocky, "No one will *know* I am a loner if there is no one here to see it."

"Then, we are in agreement. We all go. We have exactly one year to get ready and make it to the North Pole. We are gonna take the place of those stuck up North Pole reindeer, BY ANY MEANS NECESSARY!" Rocky exclaimed.

As Rocky continued speaking about how it was their time to rise to the top of the reindeer ladder, the group all heard a jingling of bells. They all looked up into the sky. There he was, Santa himself, and the reindeer pulling his sleigh. A trail of sparkling dust trailed the sleigh. They heard the feint sounds of ho…ho…ho… in the distance. A warm glow hit each of them. They all wanted to pull that sleigh, except Borris, of course, who knew that this would *never* happen. The rest thought they could do it better than the North Pole reindeer. They were determined and ready to act.

The following days were spent coming up with the plan. First, they thought about how they would get there, what to do when they got there and where *was* there exactly. Eugene suggested that they go and try to get a map from the outpost camp. He pushed up his glasses with his hoof, feeling happy with himself for coming up with such an ingenious idea. Eugene then decided to come up with an even more ingenious plan to go in and get the map, when out of nowhere, he felt a whoosh of air beside him. Everyone looked over and saw that Meteor was back, holding the map in his mouth.

Rocky looked over the map with dismay. The North Pole was a long way away, and the South Pole was surrounded by water. Eugene couldn't help but to remind everyone that the glacier was, in fact, shrinking. Laggy almost fainted when he looked at the map.

"That........would..........take.........me........100..........years..........

to..........get...there," Laggy said.

"We could get on a boat." Solo said, peeking around a snowdrift. "I saw a boat bring the men to the outpost camp. It is a big boat and I think we can hide aboard."

"What is all the uproar about and why do we need to get on a boat?" Servile asked.

"Like, we are totally going to like, the North Pole, so we can pull Santa's sleigh and get brushed and bathed and eat chocolate. Don't forget those cute little bells... they are so totally to die for!" Candy reminded Servile.

"Ok, Solo you are in charge of finding out when the boat comes and goes. Find out too if they have enough food and water aboard for us to eat and drink. You get all that Solo? SOOOLOOOO!" Rocky shouted trying to make sure Solo heard him, because he had already disappeared from sight.

Solo snuck along from snowdrift to snowdrift until he made it to the outpost camp. He listened as he heard two voices counting down something.

"9...8....7....6....5....4....3....2....1...HAPPY NEW YEAR!" the two men shouted.

"Well, this isn't my exact idea of New Years, but I can't help from being excited. You wanna know *why*?" asked Marv, knowing Henry already knew why.

"Because we leave this place in exactly ONE MONTH!" Marv yelled, with Henry joining in at the "one month" part.

"Yeah, I can't wait to get home and be with my family." said Henry, looking down at a picture of his wife and kids.

"All the tourists should be gone from New York by then, too. I mean the ball has dropped and Dick Clark has had his *Rock' in New Year's Eve* party. The whole place will be back to normal. It will just be the wife, the kids, and me. I can't wait either." Marv said with a smile.

Solo didn't wait to hear anymore. He slid around the tent, as slick as an icicle on a frozen lake. Once he was away from the tent, he moved as quickly as he could while remaining sneaky. He tried his best to stop occasionally and cover his tracks in the snow. He didn't want the men to get suspicious. When he arrived back home, he saw Rocky had the map out, puzzling over how he was going to get them there. He didn't want to let his family down.

Solo got right up behind Rocky and said, "I'm back."

Rocky jumped, slightly startled, and asked what Solo had found out. Solo explained to Rocky that the next boat would be here in a month and that the destination was New York. Rocky glanced over the map, looking for the destination, and hoped it would be on the way. He was overjoyed to find that New York would put them over halfway there. Rocky turned to Eugene and told him that once in New York, they would have to work quickly to figure out a plan for the rest of the trip. Eugene looked at Rocky from over his glasses and said it would be simple. Borris had to mention that they hadn't even *left* the South Pole yet. He reminded them of that fact every few minutes.

Laggy was put in charge of counting the supplies. He was slow, but very thorough. Borris was put in charge of gathering wood. Seeing as how there was no wood, it kept his attitude out of the way of the others, and if he didn't gather any, it didn't matter anyway. Rocky was coming up with Alpha Beta Plan Supreme. That was what he called how they would capture the other reindeer and disguise themselves. This way, they could prove that the South Pole reindeer were just as good, *if not better,* than the North Pole reindeer. The plan was simple, but sound. They would locate Santa's reindeer, capture them, and have Solo hide them. Then, they would put themselves in Santa's sleigh right before he was scheduled to leave. Finally, they would do the one night of work and reveal themselves.   Rocky already had their positions in the sleigh thought up as well. No way could Meteor lead the sleigh. He would give the rest of them heart attacks. Rocky decided Tut-tut should lead the way, followed by Laggy, Eugene, Candy, Borris, Solo and Servile. He would be in the very back with Meteor, closest to Santa, so he could hear Santa praise them endlessly.

The day finally came for the boat to bring in new people for the outpost camp. The reindeer group watched as the ship arrived. The replacements walked off the plank and immediately shook Marv and Henry's hands. The ship's crewmembers were all busy loading and unloading. The ships' captain had even come down and had a cup of coffee with Marv and Henry.

Rocky whispered to Solo, "Ok, so how do we get on?"

Solo replied, "I will take each of you on one at a time, to make sure your very well hidden."

Rocky gave him the hooves up sign and Solo got to hiding the reindeer. He started with Laggy first, who would take the longest to get in place. Laggy was almost caught when he yawned right beside a crewmember. The next one Solo hid was Tut-tut, whom he hid so well, that when he turned around, even he couldn't see where Tut-tut was. One after another after another, Solo hid them on the boat. He told each of them that he would get them food and water, because they were too noisy to even move.

Borris quickly responded with," May we breathe?" Solo snickered and replied, "No."

The boat ride was a long one, stopping at several ports to load and unload. It progressively got less and less cold, and hotter and hotter. Borris made several comments about melting and Eugene kept saying that this is what happens when reindeer don't take care of their environment. Meteor kept getting into trouble, because he couldn't keep still and would run around the boat at night. He was too quick to be seen, so Rocky didn't get too upset. Tut-tut would work on his stuttering, as usual, and that too seemed to be alright, because the crewmembers just thought something was wrong with the engine. One of the mechanics would just give the engine a whack with a wrench, which caused Tut-tut to jump, and to stop. The one that caused the most trouble onboard the ship was Servile. Mostly because he would forget where he was, and try to explore the ship. Good thing for the South Pole reindeer that Candy was always keeping her eye on everyone and was close enough in her hiding spot to look after Servile.

After what seemed to be an eternity at sea, they arrived in New York Harbor. They were several months ahead of schedule according to Eugene. Solo escorted each of them off the boat in the reverse order that they had gotten on. Rocky had a look around with Eugene and Solo, to try to determine how to get from where they were, further north. When they returned, they were shocked to discover lots of blue lights and sirens coming from the dock where they just were. They hurried back as quickly as they could, to find the other reindeer lying down asleep with small darts in their bodies. Men were loading them up in a crate. Solo tried to get closer to find out what happened. He snuck up to Borris, who was closest to them.

"Pssst! Borris, Borris." Solo whispered. "What happened?"

Borris, who was obviously under the influence of whatever was on the dart, replied, "I am going to hug Servile for asking for directions. I really am happy with him." Borris immediately lay back down and was sound asleep.

Men loaded up the captured reindeer in a crate, and Rocky overheard the men talking about taking them to the New York City Zoo. Rocky, Solo, and Eugene knew they had to do something quick, if they were to save their friends and still make it to the North Pole. Rocky looked around and noticed a huge box of multi-colored envelopes that looked just like the ones the men had back home. He motioned to Solo to go and check it out. Solo came back and said it was letters to Santa from children. Eugene smiled and said, "That box is about the same size as the one our friends are in." Rocky, Solo, and Eugene worked together to switch the address that was on the crate with the sleeping reindeer, that said TO: NY ZOO, with the one that said, TO: NORTH POLE.

Then, Solo turned to Rocky and said, "I will be right back." A few moments later, he returned with a half-smile on his face.

"You good to go?" asked Rocky, pointing to Eugene and Solo. Rocky then motioned them toward the crate and all of them got in. It wasn't a moment too soon either. Just as Rocky closed the latch, a man with a machine with two big metal teeth, came and lifted the crate.

The crate was loaded onto a truck and driven for about an hour. Rocky looked up and saw a sign, EXIT 122 Kennedy International Airport, and an arrow pointing off the road. The other reindeer were still sleeping when the truck came to a stop. They awoke rather quickly when the first aircraft's jet engine revved up beside them.

"Where are we?" asked Servile, sounding very groggy. The others looked around disoriented and wondered the same thing.

"We are at an airport. We are going to fly the rest of the way to the North Pole. Just a few more hours and we can land and begin operation Alpha Beta Plan Supreme." Rocky said, with a relieved sigh.

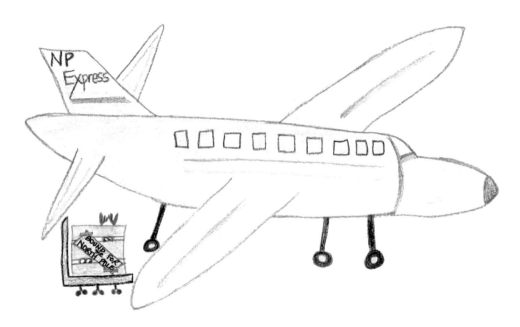

The crate was carefully loaded onto the plane and buckled down. Rocky told them to be very still and quiet, so not to arouse suspicion. They shook their heads in agreement and all of them found a comfortable spot to lie down. One of the men that loaded the plane passed by the crate and stopped for a moment.

"For letters to Santa, these letters sure smell," said the man, as he marked a check on the clipboard.

Candy stood up in a huff and pointed her hoof at the man. Quickly Tut-tut put his hoof over her mouth as she yelled muffled, "Why I never!" Tut-tut had acted just in time, as he muffled Candy's outburst, and the man just kept moving forward.

The man reached the end of the plane, most likely finishing accounting for all the cargo, when he yelled to the front of the plane to another crewmember, "Hey! I am leaving the cargo door open. Maybe we can get some of the Santa letter smell out!"

Upon hearing this, Tut-tut was about to put his hoof over Candy's mouth again, when Candy pushed it away, saying in a very quiet voice, "Maybe you should smell yourself. I *smell,* as if."

"Th-th-that's b-b-bet-t-ter C-c-candy," whispered Tut-tut.

Rocky had chosen his spot right in the front, so he could see as much as he could. The plane's engine revved even higher, and the crewmembers buckled their seatbelts. Rocky turned to the others and told them to hang on, since they didn't have any belts in the crate. Once again, the engine roared, and this time they felt the quick movement as they raced down the runway. Meteor couldn't help but let out a yelp of excitement. The men didn't notice. They were wearing headphones and the plane was way too loud. In a flash, they were in the air climbing higher and higher and higher. Rocky's stomach sank lower and lower and lower. He saw the ground starting to disappear and he quickly put his hooves to his mouth because he felt himself getting sick. Rocky began to panic, running back and forth in the crate.   Meteor thought he wanted to play, so he started running, too. Then, Rocky felt very, very, tired. Rocky fell to the floor with a thud. Solo quickly pulled out the dart in Rocky's neck.

Solo stood over him, and then turned to the others and said, "Don't worry, he is just asleep. He will be fine. The rest of you calm down, and try and be quiet."

Four hours later, the reindeer heard the crewmembers moving around in the plane. They moved the crate into position, to the back of the plane by the open door. Rocky had just woke up to hear the men talk about offloading the plane in flight.

"What does he mean off loading *in flight*?" asked Rocky in a panic. "Does that mean we don't LAND?" Rocky started racing back and forth again, and again Meteor couldn't help but join in. Rocky once again felt light-headed and sleepy. He could hear a feint laugh, that sounded like Solo, as he fell asleep.

The crewmembers checked several pieces of string that were connected to the top of the crate, and then they pushed. WHHHHOOoosh! The box fell for a bit, and then a big piece of cloth opened up, as they slowly fell to the North Pole.

When the box landed on the ground, Rocky was still asleep. Eugene told the rest of them that they weren't alone. Several small creatures were approaching from all around. Solo went and whispered something in Meteor's ear. Like a jet plane, Meteor ran out of the crate and into action.

All that could be heard was seven small voices saying, "OW!" Then, the seven small creatures fell to the ground.

Rocky awoke with a start, and jumped out of the crate. He looked around at the small creatures with pointy ears and funny shoes, all asleep in the snow, each with a dart in them. He turned and looked at Solo, who could just shrug his shoulders.

"The post cards said these were elves. Put them in the crate, so when they wake up, they won't ruin our plan. It is time, boys and girls, for Alpha Beta Plan Supreme." Rocky said, shaking the sleep from his head.

The South Pole reindeer had braved many things to this point. Now, it was time for all of their hard work to end.   They would be *the reindeer* to pull Santa's sleigh this year. Laggy, who had to be let out of the crate, because he didn't make it out by the time they put the elves in, noticed the elf footprints in the snow. They followed their footprints for a ways. Then, the light and the singing was all they needed to find Santa's home.

"All right, phase one. We scout their patterns. I just haven't figured out how we are going to knock out the North pole reindeer so we can take their place," said Rocky.

"With these," Solo said, setting nine darts on the ground in front of Rocky.

"Where did you keep all of those darts?" Rocky asked in amazement.

"Don't ask," Solo said, shaking his head.

Rocky told Solo to keep up with the darts. Solo nodded and the reindeer were off to watch and learn. The first place they went was the toyshop that was in full swing. Elves were dancing merrily and making toys. They all were so bright and happy. It looked as if they didn't want to be anywhere else in the world.

Borris took one look and said, "I will be back in the crate...asleep. Can I borrow one of those darts, Solo?"

Solo snickered and replied, "No."

Borris sighed and decided to watch the whole thing unfold anyways. He stuffed two big patches of fur in his ears, to block all the endless singing. Next, they discovered Santa's sorting room that contained the naughty and nice list. Candy looked at it with puzzlement.

"Like, do only the good people get a gift? I mean, like, so what if someone messes up just like, a little bit? I so totally don't like the naughty and nice thing. It is so like, totally bogus." Candy said in a huff, putting her nose in the air.

"Well, to be honest, I haven't found a good hiding spot yet. The elves are everywhere." Solo replied.

"I love it here! LOVE IT!" cried Meteor.

"Let's go look at where the other reindeer are." Rocky said, trying to keep the group on track.

They moved up and down the street and found a sleigh with a sign near it that read,

Practice Sleigh. They watched as the other reindeer took their places. One of the elves got inside the sleigh and called out to the other reindeer, "You all ready for flying practice?" They replied with, "Yes!"

Rocky cringed at the thought of flying away and quickly put a hoof over his mouth. The elf snapped the whip and the North Pole reindeer were off.

"Did he just whip him?!" asked Meteor. "OHHHH, heck no!! NO! NO! NO! NO! That's it. I'm done." Meteor stated, as he walked away slowly for the first time, shaking his head.

As Meteor walked away, Rocky realized that they were just not cut out for pulling the sleigh. He hung his head low and felt beaten. They had come all this way and for what? To find out that they just weren't good enough.

"What's the matter?" a jolly voice asked.

Without even looking up, Rocky replied, "The South Pole reindeer just aren't as good as the North Pole reindeer."

"HO! HO! HO! Really now, I don't believe that for a minute," the voice continued.

Rocky looked up to see Santa smiling down at him. Rocky couldn't believe it. He explained to Santa that they wanted to pull his sleigh and prove that they were just as good.

"I have been watching you the whole time, even when you were asleep. I am glad you came up here. I need reindeer who *are* afraid to fly, who are smart, who have a keen fashion sense, who complain, who are fast as the wind, who are thorough, ones who can't always fit in, and even ones who are very sneaky." Santa said, as he turned around, catching Solo sneaking up behind him with a dart in his hand.

From that day on, each of them went to work for Santa in their own way. Rocky was put in charge of all ground reindeer activities. Solo helped Santa devise new ways to sneak into homes. He even came up with an idea for an elf to go to the home before Christmas, dressed up like a doll, to open the door for Santa, since some kids don't have a chimney. Candy was put in charge of Christmas fashion. Laggy's job was to make sure the supplies for the toys never ran out. Servile became Holiday cheerleader. He didn't really get assigned this job, more than fell into it, because he always asked where he was. This made the elves burst into cheer, "The North Pole!" Eugene worked on the automation of Santa's workshop, using only biodegradable fuel to help with the "Glacier Warming" problem. Meteor actually loaded the gifts into Santa's bag, which he did faster than any elf. Even Borris would pitch in, from time to time, giving his opinions of why things were stupid. In the end, the South Pole reindeer proved they were just as good as the North Pole reindeer. They were just gifted in different ways.

So, when you leave candy and cookies for the flying reindeer, be sure to include some with a note, "These are for the *South* Pole reindeer revolt."

ABOUT THE AUTHOR

Rodney Norman is a retired Air Force veteran of twenty years. He lectured at the Air Force Technical Training school in Fort Gordon, Georgia. He holds a degree in Electronic Systems Technology from the Community College of the Air Force. He is a father of three and soon to be grandfather. He lives with his wife and youngest daughter Blair in their home in Arkansas.

Made in the USA
Lexington, KY
17 September 2017